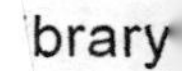

DayBlack

Written and Illustrated
by

KEEF CROSS

um Publishing

68-0544

DayBlack

by KEEF CROSS

no.1

ROSARIUM R

I never wanted them babies...Hell, I never
wanted anything those men had to offer.
But they insisted, and insisted some more,
until I was too tired to refuse. They were so
giving...They gave me pain, fear, hatred,
blood, and...my boys. I never wanted these
boys, but, since I got 'em, I'ma feed 'em,
clothe'em, shelter 'em...may even love 'em,
one day...But one thing's for sure,
when these lil boys become men,
they gon make they mama proud,
and give those men back everything
they gave to me, and a whole lot
more...

ZZZZZ
YO!
GORILLAZ
HAVE YOU SEEN
NARC
*
The same dream again...Usually, I can never remember that day, but lately, almost every detail is there. The night air, the smell of blood on cotton, and...my heartbeat...
YO!
GORILLAZ
HAVE YOU SEEN
NARC
COUP
OUTKAST
DJANGO
dead prez
Supreme

I love waking up because for a split second, I forget that I'm dead.

Climbing out of a coffin usually puts things back in perspective...

After one of my dreams, I get the urge to eat. Not because I'm hungry, but because when I dream of a time before I was turned, it makes me yearn for...well, in this case, something to chew. Something to add texture to my drink.

Yum...

MOS
DEF

MOS
I said, I yearned for something to chew. Never said anything about swallowing...

My heart hasn't beat since I was a slave, and it was beating fast with fear, just before I was bitten. Then it slowed down to nothing...

Now, *every morning*, I try to mimic those last few beats with my guitar.

When I turn on my phone, I'm greeted with groupie selfies.
Fatima

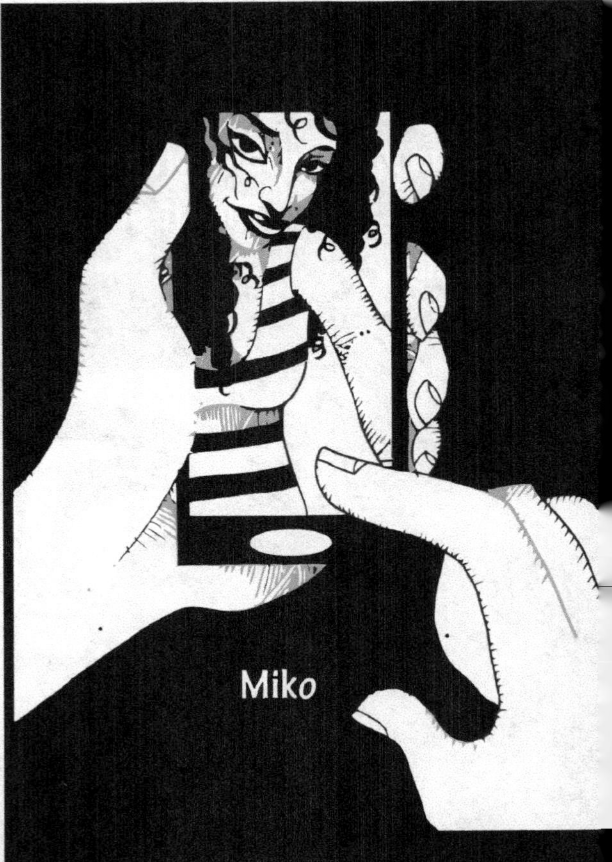
Miko

Charlene

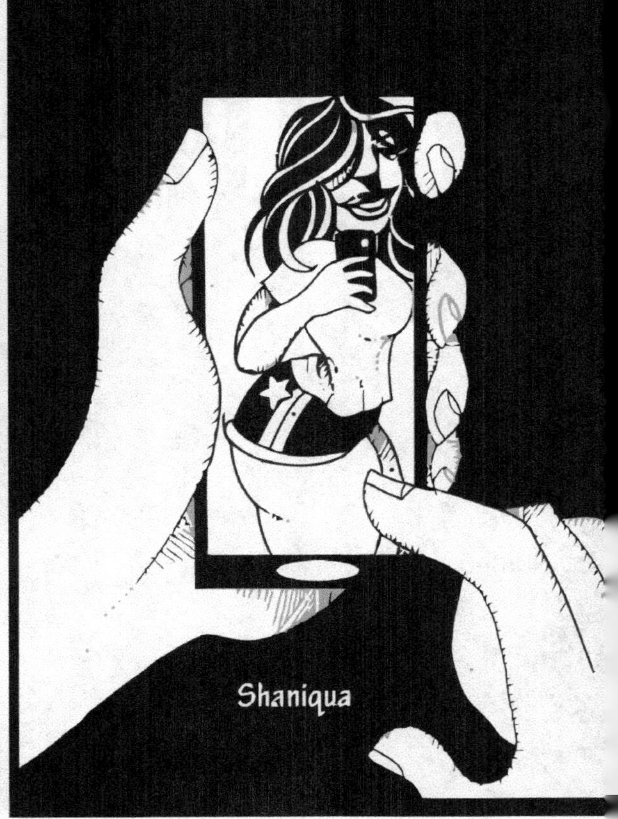
Shaniqua

I'd return the favor, but my particular condition has left me out of the social media loop.

My name is Merce,
and if you're into labels, I guess mine would be a vampire. I "live" in a small tow
in Georgia called DayBlack.

Once upon a time, DayBlack was an industrial town, but after a chemical meltdown at the steel mill, the town had to be evacuated. The only evidence left are the smokestacks that loom over the town. That, and of course the sky. The name DayBlack comes from our sky that remains black, even in the daytime, because of pollution so dense it blocks out the sun. Perfect place for me to call home. A place where there is no night or day, only DayBlack.

On my way to work, I hear the church choir singing an old spiritual that my grandmother used to sing to me.

I sit in the congregation and try to soak up all the emotions coming from the service. You can't deny the energy, no matter what you believe. I never read the bible, but i've tattooed enough scriptures that I can see where they were going with it.

You're probably wondering why I haven't burst into flames, or turned to stone or something, because of the cross. Simple...
Religious symbols only affect a vampire if it represents his religion before he was turned. For example, a cross means nothing to a vampire who was a Muslim before he was bitten. Just like the star and crescent, woudn't faze a Rastafarian.
But on the other hand, if, like me, you had no faith as a human, then symbols have no effect.

When church is over, so is the act. And people return to the gospel of needs and wants, paying tithes to the gods of rent, Jordans, and drugs. False idols, but to forsake them could mean hell on earth for some. Suddenly the energy changes,as it is known to do, and I must change with it. Starting with a change of scenery.

Living forever is like playing a video game
with all the cheat codes. Yeah, It's fun in
the beginning, but after a while, it's just
unfulfilling. Which is why , throughout my
many years , I've tried to inject some
meaning into my life sentence, trying
my hand at many professions.

Like the time when I was a mercenary...

Or that time I was an astronaut...
The stars were beautiful, but didn't seem any closer than they did in the cotton fields. I remember staring at the moon, the only witness to my transformation, as if it would shed some light on all my questions that went unanswered.

I've done it all. Currently, I've chosen the life of a tattoo artist, and I must say that, so far, it's my favorite.
How much for some stars?
must LOOK 18
YES! it hurts

I don't get to do a whole lot of custom work, mostly stars, cherries, names, shit like that. But I don't care, as long as the blood is flowing. Now, you may think you know how I get my blood, and normally you'd be right. But it's a new day. So it's not my bite that sucks them dry...

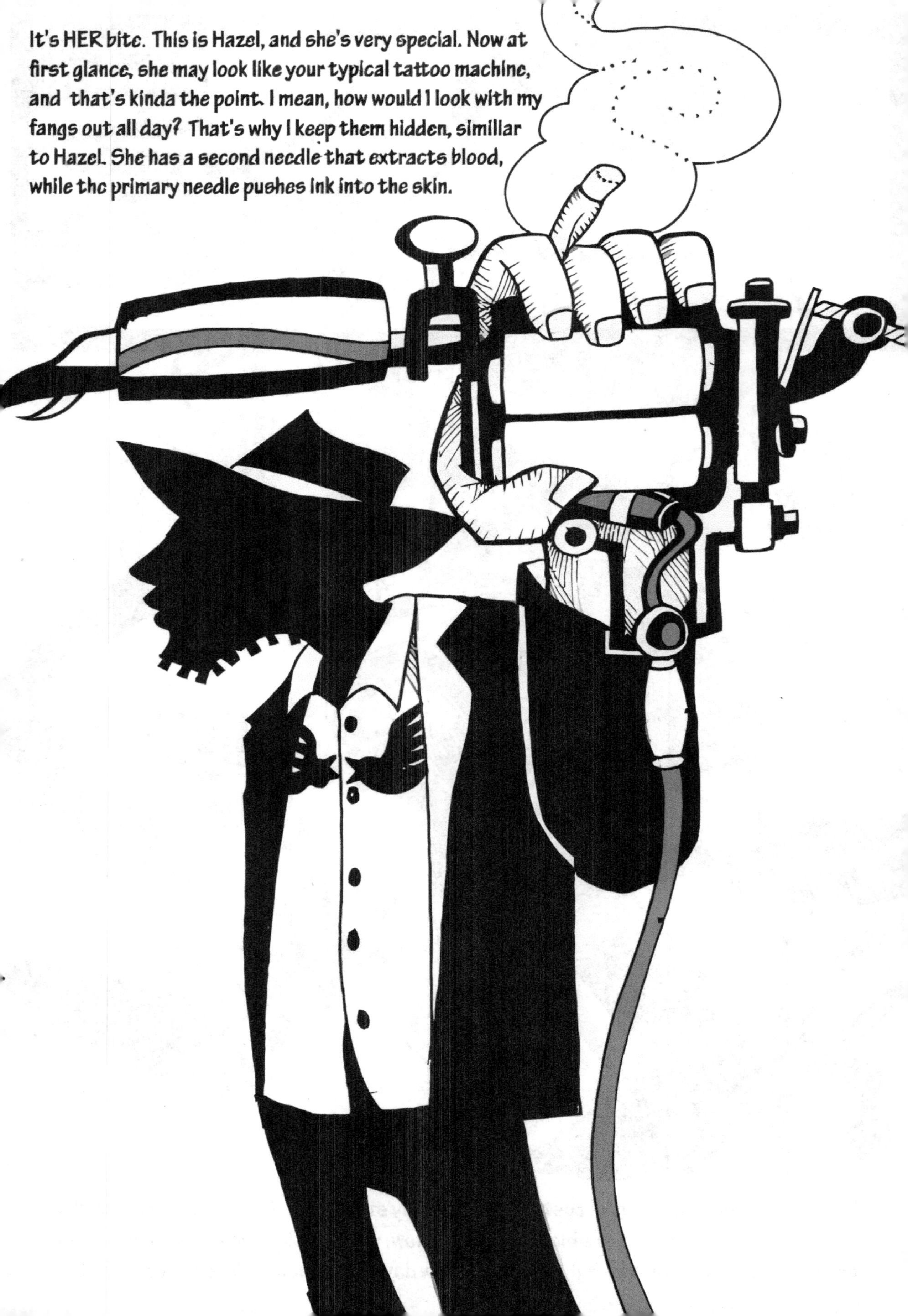
It's HER bite. This is Hazel, and she's very special. Now at first glance, she may look like your typical tattoo machine, and that's kinda the point. I mean, how would I look with my fangs out all day? That's why I keep them hidden, simillar to Hazel. She has a second needle that extracts blood, while the primary needle pushes ink into the skin.

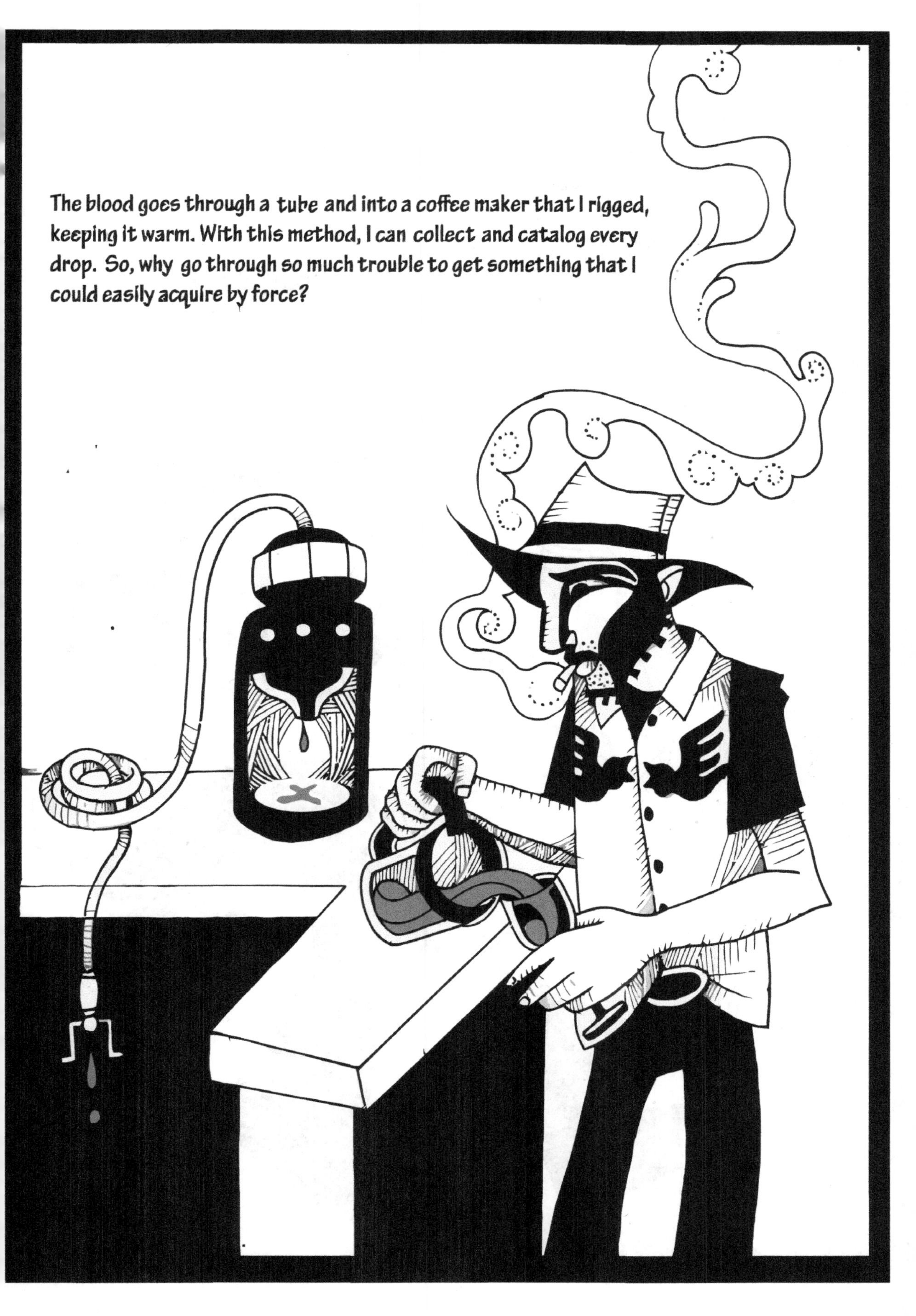
The blood goes through a tube and into a coffee maker that I rigged, keeping it warm. With this method, I can collect and catalog every drop. So, why go through so much trouble to get something that I could easily acquire by force?

Well, when H.I.V. hit the scene, vampires took the hardest hit. After all, it was intended for us. You see, when we're infected with the virus, it breaks down our ability to digest blood, making us regurgitate it, almost as soon as we drink it, thus causing us to starve to death. No longer could we just bite a random beauty. We had to take precautions to make sure blood was pure. So as the humans strapped on a collective condom, I created Hazel. Sure it's not as fun as ripping someone's jugular, and drinking blood from a glass is kinda like drinking a flat soda, but from what I hear, condoms are no fun either. Both essentially get the job done though.

So this is my "life" in a nutshell. And If you don't count the contaminated food source, and my narcolepsy (we'll get to that later), then it's a pretty simple one. Almost too simple. Sometimes I feel like a retired vampire, waiting to die somewhere in Florida. But I got this strange feeling in my gut that things are about to change...God, I hope so...

DayBlack
no.2
ROSARIUM
R

YO!
MOS DEF
dead

YO!
NARC
MOS DEF
COUP
DJANGO
dead prez

Jesus... Another dream that makes absolutely
sense.The two-headed lion was there as usual, but this time was different. I wasn't expecting to see HER there. Not that I was expecting any of it.
You talk in your sleep.
Who's Larrleux?
Look, I know we're just having fun y'know? But I really like you. I mean, I'm sleeping in a fucking coffin with you, but in your sleep you kept saying how you love this Larrleux chick. If you're hung up on her just let me know and I'll-
She was my mother.
Was?...Oh, I'm sorry. I didn't know.

Please leave.
So, can I still get my tattoo today? My husband's name?
See you at three.
YO!
NARC
MOS DEF

Larrieux...It's been so long since I've heard that
Even longer since I've heard someone other than
or my brother speak it.
YO!
NARC
HAVE YOU SEEN
dead

Larrieux, my mother, was a mute, but she always talked to me and my brother Bryce in our heads. Back then, we just thought it was another one of her spells that she was so known for. Now I know that she was a telepath.

She was called many things, but Larrieux was her true name, and only me and my brother knew it. She always said it was the only thing they couldn't take from her, so she forbade us ever speak it out loud. I loved my mother. To hear her name again gives me comfort. But to hear her name come from the lips of THAT girl, whose lips had been places I'd rather not mention, has me feeling a tad nauseous. But rather than vomiting, I'll get it out another way...

inting sometimes
ps me translate
dreams. Little
own fact, but
mpires are color
nd with the
ception of red. A
uel joke from
oever the hell made
this way. This gives us
nnel vision and sensitivity
all things red. This
why I specialize in
ck & grey tattoos with
casional red ink. Since
majority of my clients
black and brown, that's
rked out pretty good,
d when I paint, my
ette is the same.
asso had his blue
iod, so I'm in my red
iod...forever.
I'll work on this
later. Got a
feeling someth
is wrong at th
shop.

And I was right.
I don't get it! Everytime I see someone faint, it's a guy. All I did was a tear drop on his face. That means he killed someone right? So he should be a badass right? Damn, I thought men could do ANYTHING. This is sooo not gangsta.
Indeed. But my experience has shown me that women take tattoos better than me Think about it, women endu the pain of childbirth, and even a menstrual cycle is m pain than the average guy goes through. So of coure they have a higher pain tolerance. But they fain too. I think it's just more shocking to some when it's a man.
So... Who's next?
THUG

Living forever has afforded me the time to master many things. Customer service isn't one of them, and sometimes it can require a level of humanity that I simply don't possess.
That's where Mya comes in. She's my apprentice/ bartender/ anything I need her to do person.
She's fiercely loyal, and doesn't question anything I ask of her, no matter how strange the request.

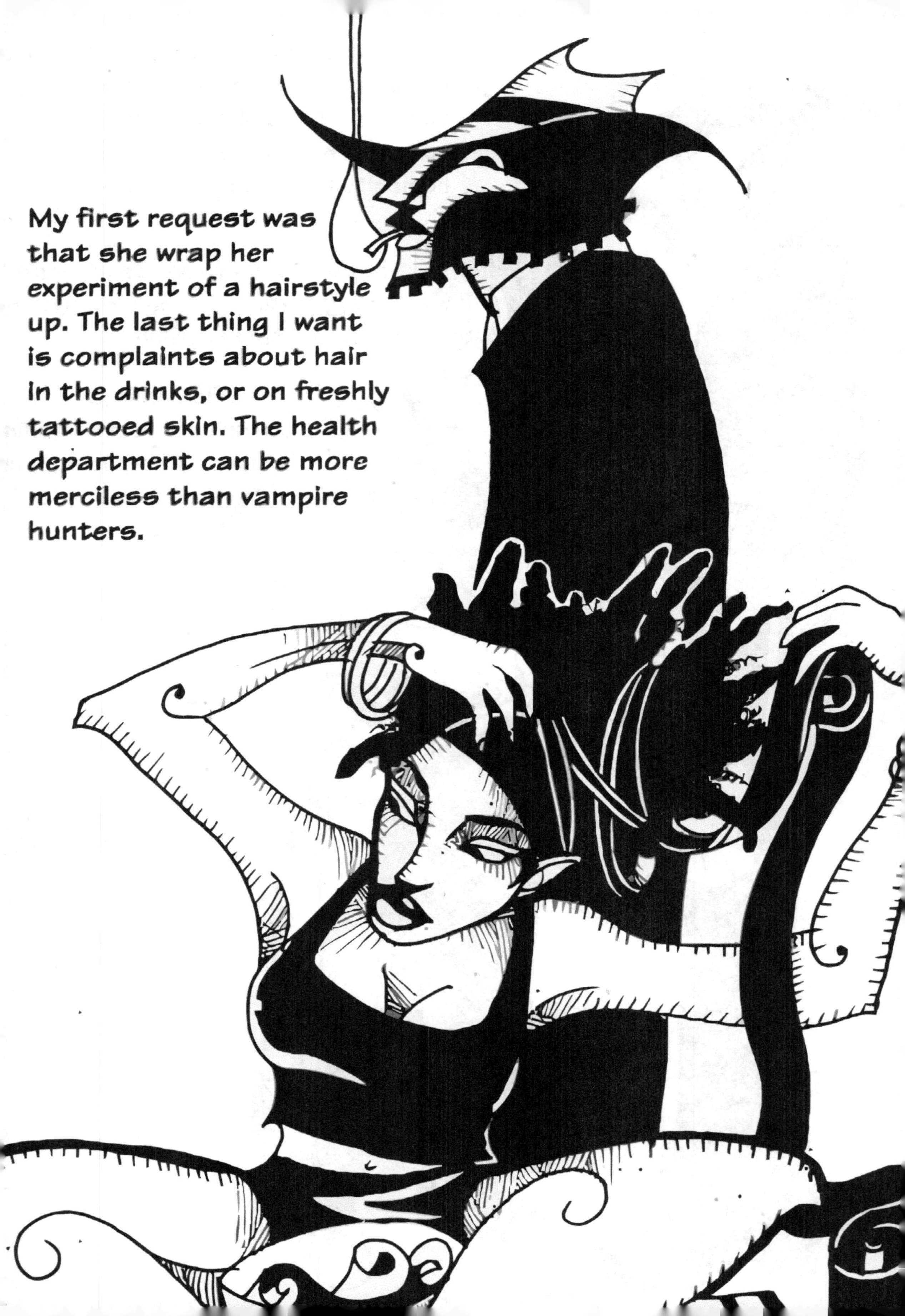
My first request was that she wrap her experiment of a hairstyle up. The last thing I want is complaints about hair in the drinks, or on freshly tattooed skin. The health department can be more merciless than vampire hunters.

Once we got that squared away, she began her apprenticeship. She's a really strong artist, and a fast learner. Unfortunately, her first lesson was that most guys will treat her like an Asian massage therapist, and want a little something extra for their buck.

But as a bartender, she's invaluable. She knows just what to say to put people at ease about getting tattooed.
Wow, I can feel your nervous energy over here. First time getting tatted?
Yeah... Everyone keeps telling me it's gonna hurt.
Don't listen to them! Every body takes pain different. Some of my tats hurt more than others. It just depends on the spot.
But you only got one tattoo.
Correction, I only have one VISIBLE tat. The rest are hidden.
But why? You work in a tattoo shop. You should be covered in tattoos!

What? You think I'm gon work here forever? And when I do leave, no tattoo is gon hold me back!
Oh.. Well I guess that makes sense.
Doesn't it? So where are you getting your tattoo?
On the top of my head.
AWWW NEGRO! That's bout to hurt!!!

My first customer of the day is Vick. Part-time paramedic, full-time heroin addict. He provides me with blood from the hospital during the slow season, and in exchange I cover the track marks on his arm, and believe me, it's steady work. A tattoo artist sometimes plays the role of a poor man's shrink, as I listen to Vick spill his junkie guts, inflicting and absorbing pain simultaneously. Today he's getting a portrait of a woman that died on his shift.

I'd been using needles from the ambulance to shoot up with all week! There was only one left, and it was in my pocket. Can you believe it?
see where this is going.
See, I'd just got some really sweet stuff from my guy, so good he calls it HEAVEN. When I got off work, I was gonna go home, and put the world on mute! So... I made a choice.

It was the wrong choice. I let that lady die...But I've done worse. You know how I'm living. So what are your thoughts Merce?
Well, it sounds like she went to heaven so you could go to heaven.
Aww man, that's fucked! But I kinda like the sound of it. Matter fact, put that in the tat, right over her head!
"She went to heaven, so that I could go to heaven."
Loser
I was joking...

fter I finish tattooing a dead woman's face, and making light of it with er killer, a part of me bathes in the irony, splashing around in it like a hild in a kiddie pool. But then there's that other part that needs a palette leanser. No such luck with my next client Vera.

On days like this I move through the crowd, quiet, unnoticed. I don't care who was next, or how long they've waited, I pick my next customer by who has the loudest blood flow...And this crowd sounds like Niagara Falls. Certain variables also influence who I choose to tattoo next.
YES!
iPS

For instance, a skinny girl will get skipped over.
Simply because getting blood from her is like trying to suck a milkshake through a narrow ass straw. Your face will cave in...

Which is why I prefer
a wide mouth straw...
JAMAICA
If their blood
checks out after
the tat, then I
can drink directly
from a thick
chick all night
without draining
her.

idway through my next tattoo, I start to feel it happening...
Whoah, Somebody had a long night. You're not gonna fall asleep on me are you?
YAAAWN! Naw baby, fall asleep, while I'm tatting? That... Would...Be...
...Crazy...

Shit! Sleep again...
I have no control at
this point as to
where my mind
will take me.
They always
start off very
bizzare, before
they even out
into something
more logical.
Simillar to
a space
shuttle
re-entering
earth's
atmosphere.
It must
burn first.

Ok, this is more like it. I remember this day.
I remember...her...
Why you like working at nigh all the time?
I'd rather work under the moon than the sun.
Smart. I'll call you Moon Man.
Hahaha
Must be nice, having a choice of when to work. The rest of us gotta work in that hot ass sun till we bout to fall out! I always bring you water, but you're never there. Now I know why. Yo daddy must be white, getting all that special treatment.
I don't know. I never met him.
I never met my daddy either, but I'm sure his ass ain't white! Hahahaha!!
I KNOW you didn't fall asleep on my tattoo!!
WHAT??!

Huh?
Hold up! I KNOW you didn't just fall asleep in the middle of doing my tat!
Aw hell naw, wait till I tweet this! You'll never tattoo in this town again!!
If people found out that I fall asleep during tattoos, that would be the end of my business, and the beginning of me getting my blood the old way. I can't let that happen
So what I do?

up, you guessed
As her heart takes its last beats, I hold her close, and imagine her heart is mine.

That's the third tin this month I've falle asleep during a tat I've always had the dreams, but it's ne affected my work. Now it seems to b happening more frequently, and t dreams are gett stranger and stranger.
I didn't wanna kill her, and if I knew how good she tasted, I would've thought twice, but social media has left no room for error, and rumors spread faster than wildfire. Shame though, she would've loved her tattoo...

Like the time I dreamed a dragon was choking me with its tail.
SPELMA

Or the time I dreamed that
I tattooed the Devil...
OOOOWWW
IT BURNS!!
Jesus
Christ

Hell, I can't even get a lapdance without dozing off.

To kill.
Or not to kill.
When I killed for blood, I had no problems.
Since I started my ne feeding method, I've become a narcoleptic with dreams nuttier than squirrel shit.
I'll have to smoke on that later.
For now, I gotta get rid of this body.

e record, vampires don't dig graves. We kill an keep it
g. But being that I'm the sole
re in DayBlack, I must
my tracks, lest I
acked and
d.

Took you long enough to dig this grave Vampire.
Speak of the devil.

You ready to
to lie in it?
TBC

3
DayBlack
R
CROSS

That's right, for only 89 cents a day, the price of a cup of coffee, you can feed, clothe, and shelter children like little Rodamez here. His parents were killed in a home invasion. So many children have been orphaned and forced to join violent cartels before they even learn to read. But with a little help from people like you, little Rodamez can have a new outlook on life.
I ♥ NY

I know you're at home, sitting on your couch wondering, "How can I make a difference?" For starters, pick up the phone and let one of our operators tell you how your pocket change can change a child's life.
So I did. I don't know why, but there was so much pain and hate in this kid's eyes that even I was moved.

So I picked up the phone and began my long distance adoption of young Rodamez. I send money, and they send me photos and progress reports. Sometimes I would get letters from Rodamez himself. Watching his English get better with each letter gave me a feeling of fulfillment that was foreign to me.
Mean little bastard...
When he became fluent in English, he was able to better articulate the horrors he had witnessed and been victim to. With each letter, I knew I had done the right thing.
But as the years passed by like seconds, I noticed the letters stop coming, and I stopped expecting them. What became of little Roda I wondered. Had he been slain in some shantytown or sold into chil slavery or worse? Then one day my answer came in the form of a...
KNOCK KNOCK

When I opened the door...
Yes we're OPEN
I have waited a very long time to meet the person who looked down on me with mercy, when even GOD would not, and reached out their hand to help instead of hurt...
To give me a fighting chance in this life... Father.

Sure he got older, but the eyes were exactly the same...

He told me of his master ,Bolo, aka The Brown Recluse. Bolo was once a Black Panther, who tried to get the brothers to turn their attention and resources from fighting the white man to fighting a bigger threat to all mankind, vampires. Of course he was ejected from the Panthers. So he took all his weapons and expertise to Mexico and began training some of the most legendary hunters. When Rodamez found him, he had been long retired and beaten by alcohol. But after hearing Rodamez's story, he accepted the boy's weekly offerings of food, alcohol, and Black Tail nudie mags in exchange for a hunter's apprenticeship.

Use your blade for intimidation! Let your opponent believe your deadliest weapon is your knife. So when he is cut by your fist, it is a revelation to him!

Breath control is essential to stealth. They can hear you breathing a mile away. Remember, shorter breaths, quicker steps!
I filled the tub with pig's blood because you may find yourself choking on your own blood one day. This will help.

time has come.
I've taught you not
all that I know, for
hat would be foolish,
ut rather all you need
o know. Ivory is the
ue killer of the vampire,
ot the wooden stake.
he leopard walrus has
vory tusks. Your final
ask will be to go to the
Great White Nothing
and bring the beast's
tusks to me.

After days of waiting in the Great White Nothing, Rodamez began to feel the nag of starvation, making his senses more acute. He soon forgot why he was there. All that mattered now was survival.
That's when the walrus revealed himself.

Then everything went black.

When he came to, the walrus was dead.

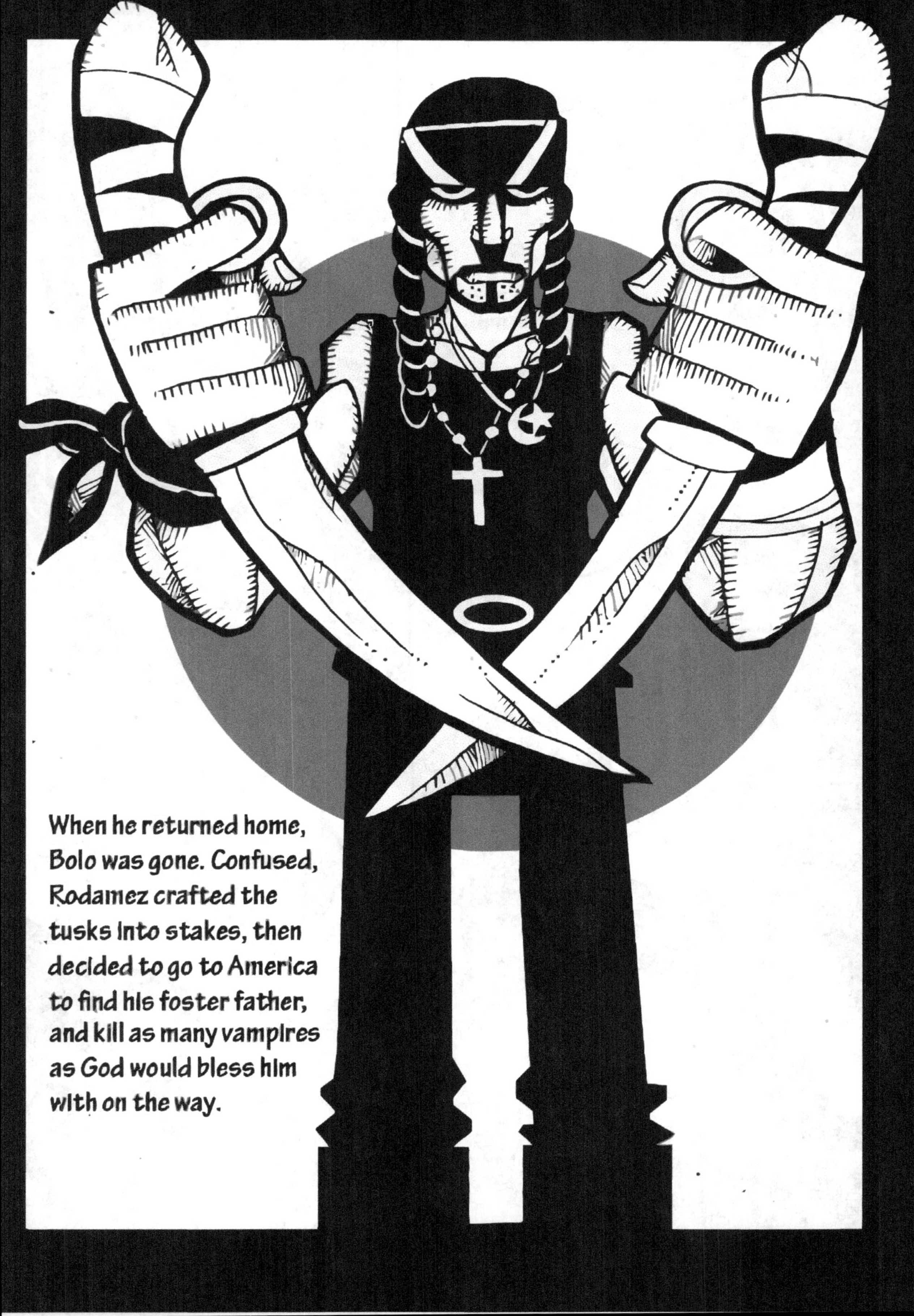
When he returned home, Bolo was gone. Confused, Rodamez crafted the tusks into stakes, then decided to go to America to find his foster father, and kill as many vampires as God would bless him with on the way.

God Is good

So basically, I paid for vampire killing college. But now I was his "Father" right? So we sealed our newly found with a tattoo. This was the first time Rodamez had been this close to a vampire that he wasn't killing and my first time around a hunter, so things were a little tense at first.

I guess you can buy a lot for the price of a cup of coffee a day.

Thought you were a goner, eh old man?
Now I see my "son" standing over me, stakes drawn. We're talking about a guy who has devoted his life to killing people like me for doing what I just did. But being his foster dad, I get a pass.
So... Who's getting planted?
Trust me, it was necessary. What brings you to town?
Following a trail. I've been tracking two vampires across the country for months, but when I saw where they were headed, I knew I had to end it here. A town without sunlight. DayBlack could become a vampire mecca. Without the sun, our cause would be lost.

eir "cause". I really couldn't care less.
at worries me is a town full of vampires.
ey would suck this town dry. That can't
ppen.
Anything I can do to help?
Try not killing anyone. More hunters are coming, and I won't be able to protect you. Hovering in public?
Yeah, knock that shit off, too.

The great Rodamez needs back up? They must be a couple of vicious bastards.
Oh, and another thing, I never told you this, but under the circumstances, you should know. All hunters are of Mexican descent. Most of us come here because America has the highest concentration of vampires in the world.
Of course I knew this already, like most vampires but sometimes it's best to be quiet and listen, and let humans think they know something we don't. We let them believe that wooden stakes could kill us for millennia...That was pretty funny.
No shit?

As our cover, we take jobs most Americans won't do, being paid next to nothing. Most commonly we work as landscapers because our tools-machetes, chainsaws and such-are readily available without question.

If you get a call in the next few days about a complimentary lawn treatment, prepare yourself.
I'll be in touch.
As if I didn't have enough on my mind. Vampires in my town and hunters on the way. This is no time for me to let my guard down, and my narcolepsy may be a liability.

I pay a visit to one of my donors. Her name is Empress, a pharmacist with a habit of taking her work home with her...
I need a prescription filled, ASAP.
Damn Merce, you can't just be popping up on me like that!
Can't I? Or can I come and go as I see fit? Now, I need something to keep me awake and alert. What's on the menu?
I don't have time to argue wit her, so I offer a "suggestion"
Of course, love. I'll see if White Girl Abbey is home.

Our usual agreement is, in exchange for tattoos, Empress allows me to drink from her while she's under the influence of whatever drug I'm in the mood for. Feeding this way allows me to experience the same high or low that she does. This is the only way a vampire can feel the effects of drugs.
Nesta

I give the drugs time to work their way into her bloodstream, and then I take a hit.
White Girl Abbey is a combination of cocaine and Adderall that Empress assures me will keep me at attention for days.
She takes a lethal dose, but I drain her just enough to keep her from overdosing.
I fall asleep almost immediately...

When I wake up, I head to my favorite spot for a much needed distraction...

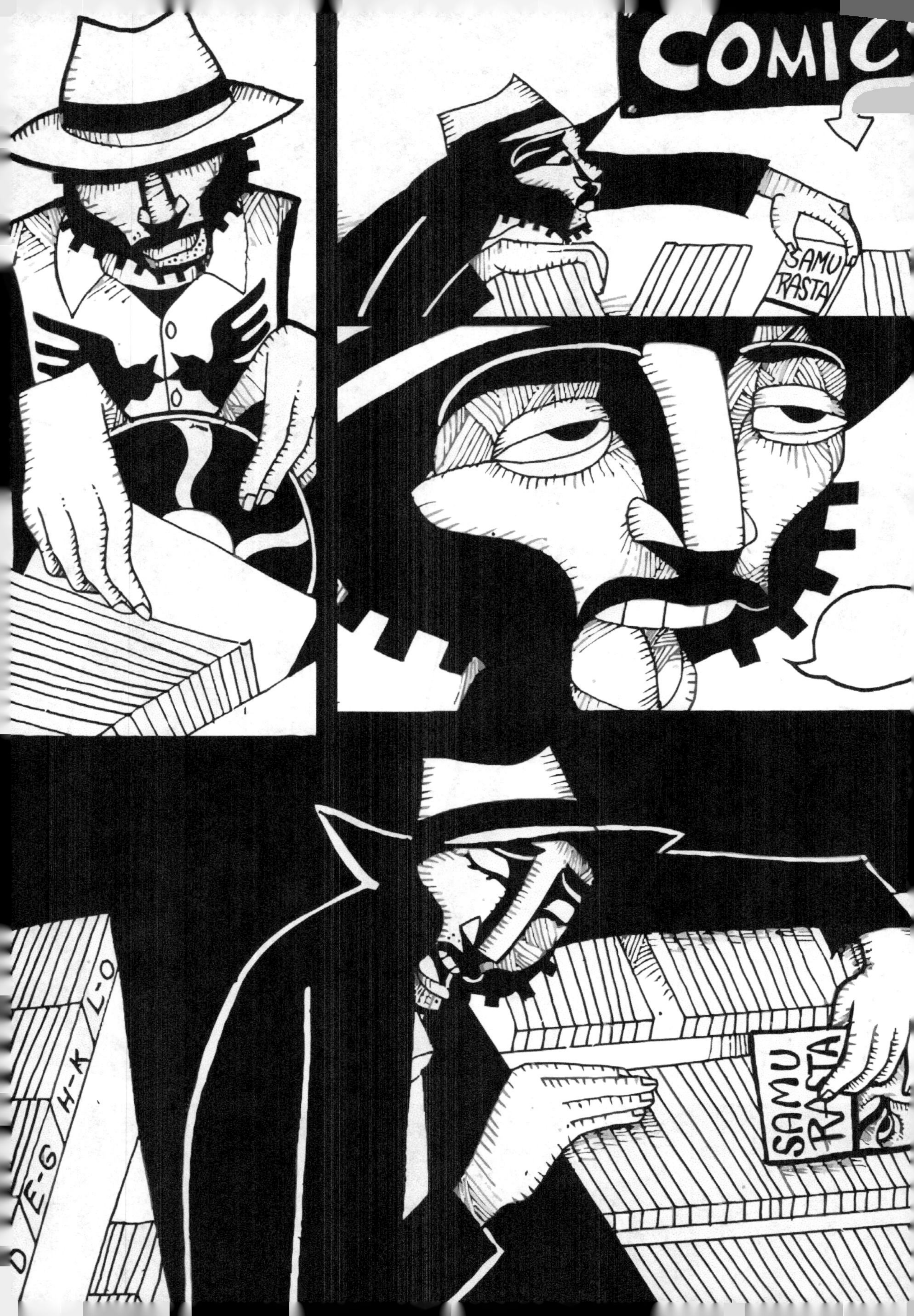
COMIC
SAMU RASTA
D
E-G
H-K
L-O
SAMU RASTA

SAMU
RASTA

Merce! Merce, wake up man! You snoring loud as hell bruh!
*
ZANO
SAMU RASTA
Rest man, you need some.
You know, living in a place like this where there's no daytime, can kinda screw with you. Some days I don't know when the hell to go to sleep. This gonna be it for you?
YUP.
ZANO
CASH ONLY
RUN THE JEWELS
Green Day
RAMONES

¿Vampiro, que haces afuera en el sol?
He said, what are you doing walking around in the daytime, vampire?

"Don't take us for fools. When we saw you asleep, I tried to film you fo
World Star, but you didn't show up on my phone.
COMICS
COMICS
E-6
Vampire? Do you mean me, sir?
That's right! I'm a magician, and you've just seen my first trick of the evening. Now for my next mind blowing feat, I will give one of you gentlemen the most painful heartburn you've ever experienced.

Don't tell me...You've seen this trick before.
Mi hermano...

It's been so long since I was attacked by a human, I forgot how slow they are.
¡VAMPIRO
But they always regroup pretty fast

Umm...You...
You can't...You
can't bring pets
in here...
Better let it
slide Zano. You might
wanna close early and get
outta here. But first, throw
on some M.O.P. I'm gonna
need some theme
music.

DAY BLACK
@TorrenceReed
John Jennings

FLASH
by
MERCE

dayblack
FLASH
by
MERCE

FLATBUSH YARD
#1

21st Century Gods

David Tallerman

Duncan Kay

MANTICORE
ROSARIUM
R
Issue One
KEITH
A. MILLER
IAN
GABRIEL

ALSO FROM ROSARIUM!!!

in
OVENLAND

RosariumPublishing.com